THIS BOOK BELONGS TO

Gyo Fujikawa's
Oh, What a Busy Day!

GROSSET & DUNLAP • PUBLISHERS • NEW YORK
A FILMWAYS COMPANY
1978 Printing
Library of Congress Catalog Card Number: 76-4259. ISBN: 0-448-12511-0 (Trade Edition); ISBN: 0-448-13369-5 (Library Edition). Copyright © 1976 by Gyo Fujikawa.

I'm up! I'm up!
It's going to be a busy day...
Must brush my teeth,
wash my face, comb my hair,
and get dressed...

Then a great, big breakfast!

Through the teeth,
Past the gums,
Look out, stomach!
Here it comes!

Mother, dear,
I sadly fear,
My appetite
is always here!

THEN WE GO OUT TO PLAY

Run, rush,
   chase and scramble.
Sing, shout,
   laugh and giggle!

Hop, skip,
   dance and dawdle.
Fight, cry,
   make up and smile.

Flip, flop,
   upsy-daisy!
Stop! Chat!
   Gossip a bit!

Bounce, bounce,
  bounce, little ball,
Up, down,
  don't bounce away!

Let's sing!
  La-di-da-da!
  Let's not!
  Yakety-yak-yak!

One, two,
  buckle my shoe.
Let's play
  Hide-and-Go-Seek!

Bushel of wheat, bushel of barley,
All not hid, holler "Charley!"

Bushel of wheat, bushel of rye,
All not hid, holler "I!"

More things to do
in
    back yards,
    front yards,
    playgrounds,
and
    country meadows!

Well, what do you know?
It's raining!
We'll have to play indoors!

So here we are!
Indoors!
I know what I'm going to do!
Do you?

Guess What?

Do you ever pretend that
you are something or
someone you're not?

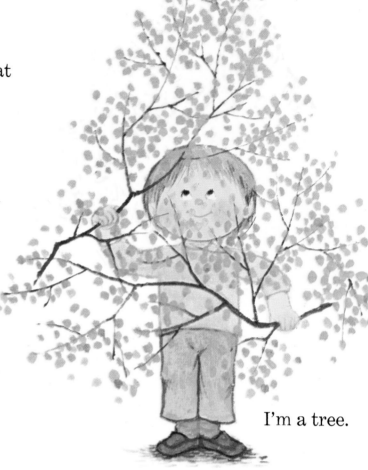

I'm a tree.

Quack! Quack! I'm a duck.

I'm a queen.

I'm Santa Claus.

I'm a sandwich.

I'm a dinosaur.

I'm a peacock.

I'm a house.

I'm a robot.

I'm a turtle.

BEST FRIENDS

Do you have a best friend?
A one and only
really true friend?
I do!
  She's Jenny!
  And she's my very best friend!

Best friends
  like best
to be with each other,

to talk and play,

and joke
  and laugh
    at the same things!

Now and then,
    best friends quarrel,
    or even have a nasty
        knock-down fight!

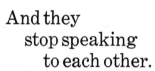

And they
    stop speaking
        to each other.

But then,
    they can't stay mad…
so they make up,
    happy to be best friends again.

Sometimes,
    Jenny and I
        don't talk at all.
We don't have to.
    She knows what I'm thinking
        and I know
            what she's thinking!

Right now,
    Jenny is thinking,
"Let's go
    and work
        in the garden!"

And I
    am thinking
        the very same
            thing!

We dig the earth
   and ply the hoe.
   We plant the seeds
   and watch them grow.

The sun and rain
   will help the seeds
   to bud and sprout
   and thrive like weeds.

Then snap a bean,
   sniff geraniums,
   munch a carrot,
   or snip nasturtiums.

SUSIE'S SECRETS

I know some secret hiding places
I'll not tell another person!
Never,
    never,
        never!

I found out where
the tiny mouse
hurries away to...but
I'll never tell!

I also discovered
    where Major likes
to hide...but
    don't worry,
    I won't tell!

The little brown bird
hopes no one will find
her nest... I did, but
I'll never tell!

Pussy cat doesn't like
to be disturbed
when she's hiding... so
I'll never tell!

I know where to look
when little brother
hides... well,
I won't tell ...
but I won't promise!
Ha, ha, ha!

And then there's my own
top-secret place.
Don't ask me where,
for I'll not tell.
It's my very own,
my secret
hideaway!

WHEN I'M GROWN UP!

I think I'll be a
ski jumper!

I'm going to be a
tap-dancer.

A football
star!

A clown.

Guess what
I want to be?

I'd love to be a
mountain climber.

An author?

And what do *you* want

A fireman?

A cowboy?

A teacher?

A veterinarian?

A nurse?

An opera singer?

A doctor?

A fisherman?

o be when you grow up?

A construction
worker?

A policewoman?

A pilot?

A ballet dancer?

A cook?

A farmer?

An artist?

A pop singer?

An animal trainer?

I'm going to be ME!

Hold on, Mrs. Pussycat!
I'll save your kitten!

KINDNESS

How many kind thoughts
   can a little child have
   for others?

How many kind deeds
   can a little child do
   for others?

How many can you count?
   I'm sure there are a
   hundred and one ways!

How do you feel this morning?

Poor lost dog! ... Don't worry, I'll find your home for you!

Come, take my hand!

Oops! Let me help!

And a long time ago, Christina Rosetti wrote,

The dear old woman in the lane
    Is sick and sore with pains and aches,
We'll go to her this afternoon,
    And take her tea and eggs and cakes.

We'll stop to make the kettle boil
    And brew some tea and get the tray,
And poach an egg, and toast a cake,
    And wheel her chair around, if we may.

SUMMERTIME

Rock in a hammock.
Go on a hike.
Dunk in a pool.
Have a picnic.
Sleep in a tent.

Lemon juice
  and sugar.
Lots of water,
  lots of ice.

Stir them all
  together.
Stir and swirl them
  all around.

And presto!
  like magic!
It's puckery,
  delicious,
  ice-cold
  lemonade!

IT'S VERY SAD

when good friends must say goodbye,

when puppy is sick,

when dolly breaks her head,

when you're afraid kitty is lost,

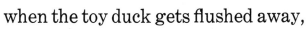

when the toy duck gets flushed away,

and when it pours rain on your picnic.

And here is a very, very sad story . . .

THE BABES
IN THE WOOD

My dear, do you know,
How a long time ago,
    Two little children,
Whose names I don't know,
Were stolen away,
On a fine summer's day,
    And left in a wood,
As I've heard people say?

Among the trees high
Beneath the blue sky
    They plucked the bright flowers
And watched the birds fly;
Then on blackberries fell,
And strawberries red,
    And when they were weary,
"We'll go home," they said.

And when it was night,
So sad was their plight,
    The sun it went down,
And the moon gave no light.
They sobbed and they sighed,
And they bitterly cried,
    And the poor little things
They lay down and died.

And when they were dead,
The robins so red
    Brought strawberry leaves
And over them spread;
And all the day long,
The green branches among,
    They'd prettily whistle.
And this was their song:
"Poor babes in the wood!
Sweet babes in the wood!
    Oh, the sad fate of
The babes in the wood!"

BRAND NEW BABIES

Hello, brand-new baby!
How do you do!
Welcome! Welcome!

Hurry and grow up,
so you can play ball with us!

Waaaah!

Waaaah!

Waaaah!

My goodness!
There are three new babies
all at once at our house!

Babies need lots of love and attention!

Sometimes, big brother gives a helping hand.

They never seem to guzzle enough milk!

It's fun to watch baby get bigger and bigger!

Sleep, little friend, sleep—
    When morning comes,
    I'll be here
    to make you laugh
at my hippity-hop, hop, and hop.

IT'S OKAY

It's okay if you're naughty
and mischievous and mean—
sometimes...But later,
don't forget to say "I'm sorry!"

And once in a while, it's okay
to pout and sulk and be cross,
But you'll agree that
you look pretty ugly! Right?

It's all right to mope around,
looking wretched and woebegone.
Occasionally, that is.
    It's okay!

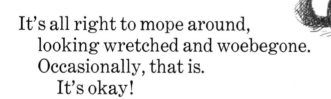

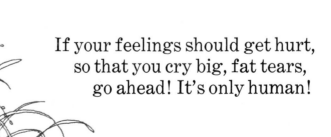

If your feelings should get hurt,
so that you cry big, fat tears,
go ahead! It's only human!

It's okay if you're bashful
    and tongue-tied, shy, and blushing.
There are lots of people
    Just as bashful as you and I.

After a bad dream,
    isn't it good to wake up
    and know that
    everything's okay?

And it's disgraceful, but
    it's okay to squabble once
    in a while. (Although
      hardly ever would be better!)

But what can we do
    about terrible
    temper tantrums?

Happiness is a
        gooey mud puddle!
It's okay!
        Jump up and down!
        Splash! Wallow!
        Squish your toes!
Wow!

Christopher Columbus,
What do you think of that?
A big, fat lady
sat on my hat!

Hi, ya, Joe!
What d'ya know?

Oh, Marguerite,
go wash your feet!
The Board of Health's
across the street.

Smarty,
Smarty,
thought you
had a
party!

I scream,
you scream.
We all scream.
for ice cream.

I should worry,
I should care,
I should marry a
millionaire!

Ed, Ed,
has a
big head!

Monkey, monkey,
sittin' on a rail.
Pickin' his teeth
with the end of his tail!

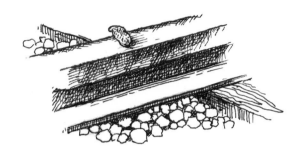

A peanut sat on a railroad track,
His heart was all a-flutter;
Along came a train—the 9:15—
Toot, toot! Peanut butter!

Open your mouth
   and shut your eyes;
And I'll give you something
   to make you wise.

If you are a honest child,
As I think you be,
You'll neither smile nor giggle
When I tickle your knee.

A big bumblebee
Sat on a wall;
He said he could hum,
And that was all.

Betty Boop,
   Ain't she cute?
All she says is
   "Boop boop-a-doop."

Cry, baby, cry,
Stick your finger in your eye;
If your mother asks you why,
Tell her that you want some pie.

Fuzzy-Wuzzy was a bear
Fuzzy-Wuzzy had no hair,
Fuzzy-Wuzzy wasn't fuzzy,
Was he?

I DON'T EITHER!

Rose, Rose,
   has big toes;
She carries them
   wherever she goes.

Lift the nozzle
   to your muzzle,
And let it swizzle
   down your guzzle.

"Flying man, flying man,
    Up in the sky,
O where are you going,
    Flying so high?"

"Over the mountains
    And over the sea!"
"Flying man, flying man,
    Can't you take me?"

We Love Animals

See how many animals you can name!

TURN THIS PAGE
TO SEE
A DREAM COME TRUE
FOR SOME
ANIMAL LOVERS...

WHEN COLD WINDS BLOW

Red leaves
        rustle,
Red leaves
        bustle,
Red leaves
        spin,
October's
            in!

Little witches,
    Little ghosts,
Scaring folks—
    themselves the most!

Wintery winds,
whirling snow.
Icy, shivery,
shuddery,
bleak.
Winter winds,
go away!

Stay here...
so warm,
cozy,
and toasty!

It stopped!
It's gone!
    The chilly blasts!
Hooray!
    Where's my hat?
    Where's my coat?
C'mon, everybody...
    Let's go!

It's wintertime! It's snowtime!
So get your sleds,
your skates, and snowshoes.
We'll slide and glide and
mush the whole day long!

A FEW CHARMS AND WISHES

Star light, star bright,
  First star I see tonight.
I wish I may, I wish I might,
  Have the wish I wish tonight.

Break it short,
bad luck!
Break it long,
good luck!

He loves me,
  he loves me not.
He loves me,
  he loves me not.

A four-leaf clover for good luck!

Lady Bird, Lady Bird,
    Fly away home.
Your house is on fire.
    Your children are gone.

Touch blue,
my wish will
come true!

See a pin, pick it up.
    All day long you'll have good luck.
See a pin, let it lay.
    You'll have bad luck all that day.

Step on a crack,
    You'll break your mother's back.

Blow out the candles
    with one great WHOOH!
And positively,
    your wish'll come true!

Cross my heart,
    and hope to die,
If I should tell
    A big, fat lie!

I DON'T WANT TO PLAY ANY MORE

All day long
   we played together
   and talked of many things.
We had such a good time!
But now, I'm tired.
I want to go home.
So, so long!
   See you tomorrow!

And then, finally,
there's sunset time,
almost suppertime;
the quiet time of day.

And now,
  It's bedtime.
How nice it'll be
  to stretch
  and rest
  and sleep...
It has been such
  a busy,
  busy day!